FRUSTRATION

Abiodun Felix Taiwo

FRUSTRATION

(A collection of short stories)

Abiodun Felix Taiwo

For further information or permission, contact;

felixtaiwo660@yahoo.com

DEDICATION

This book is dedicated to the Almighty God for His infinite mercies upon my life and my family as well.

ACKNOWLEDGEMENT

I would not have achieved this without the encouragement and immense support of my wife, Mrs. Tolulope.

To my children, Ayodimeji, Oluwakanyinsola and Ifeoluwa, you've ensured the home was a peaceful and conducive environment for me to study and write, I appreciate you guys for this

TABLE OF CONTENTS

INTRODUCTION

The stories in this collection are all about frustration and disappointment. Frustration is an emotion that comes from disappointment. It is the feeling of being disappointed or discontent with something or someone, usually because you expected more. Frustration can also be caused by something that is not working properly or is broken down.

In this collection, the author explores the different ways in which frustration can play out in relationships between people, or even within ourselves. We see how it causes us to act irrationally or do things we regret later on because we were so caught up in our emotions at that moment.

In The Water Pump, the author tells a story of a broken friendship and the disappointment that led to it and that ensued afterwards. A Lesson in Irony is indeed a lesson about how things seem to go the way they shouldn't and how frustration can come out of that. A Tale of Failurc tells how frustration can lead to depression and what we should not do to push people over the edge.

Frustration is something we can all relate to. These stories are an attempt to show how frustration can lead us down many different paths, whether it be disappointment in ourselves or others or just general anger and confusion about life. This collection of short stories will take you on a journey through life's journey as seen through the eyes of three different characters who represent different types of people. Each has their own unique way of dealing with their struggles and frustrations, but one thing is for sure: these stories will inspire you to be better than you were before.

THE WATER PUMP

CHAPTER ONE

WHAT HAPPENED AT THE WATER PUMP?

For Alani and Tola and I, the water pump was a place of impressive memories. It was at the water pump that Alani and I had our first fight, that fateful fight over who should fetch water into their bucket next that led to us becoming friends. Tola stood by the whole time and after a while, she started separating us, something other people around dared not to do because we two were considered the strongest boys in the neighbourhood. And there were no elders around to curtail us from fighting. Tola picked up a weak stick and started hitting both of us, even as everyone cautioned her to stop.

'You don't separate a fight between two angry boys,' they said, but she continued. And then we stopped fighting altogether. We both faced her. In fear, she dropped his stick and ran off. But she had completed her mission that we stop fighting.

That day went by as though it were an ordinary day, except one with just the fight of young boys. Moreover, which day was there not to fight in the neighbourhood?

The next time I went to play football, I ended up being in the same team as Alani and we had to play together. I was confused as to why. Where has this boy come from? How did he land in our village? I had never seen him before. He didn't even attend my school, which is, of course, the only secondary school in the village. So, after the match, we got talking.

"Who are you? Where have you come?" I asked. Alani replied that he was a son of our Williamson town, but his parents had travelled off for a long time since he was young. However, now he had been brought back to live with his grandmother to see out his education. Apparently, there was no secondary school in his parents' village. Therefore, he must live with his grandmother for the time being.
After our discussion, we shook hands. And from then on our friendship slowly blossomed. I introduced him to Tola, who was the most brilliant student in our class. And he, in turn, taught me some football tricks that I was not familiar with.

It turned out that every evening, we would meet at the water pump: the lone giant water pump in the village to fetch water for our homes. Of course, all the children gathered there every evening, carrying buckets and jerrycans and bowls to fetch water for their families. But for Alani and I, we had a specific spot away from all the action near the water where we talked and talked about life while we waited for our turn to get water.

One day Tola found us in our subtle hideout, and she came over, teasing, "So this is where you guys come to hang out, right? What are you up to?" Her mood was light-hearted away from the fight we had the other day and Tola seemed particularly pleased that I and Alani had grown to become friends.

She patted us lightly on the back and said, "my good boys." We laughed heartedly.

From then on, it had to become a tradition for Alani and Tola and me to hang out at the water pump almost every other day. It was a place where we formed tight bonds of friendship. It was the place where we shared deep secrets about each other. It was a place where we gossiped. The only thing we didn't do at the water pump was study, because, of course, it was under a tree. Where would we read? But every other thing we could do? We did. We told each other about our crushes in school. We told each other about teachers we liked and teachers we didn't like. We talked about everything and anything we could talk about. The water pump was really a place of memories for us.

CHAPTER TWO
DISUNITY AT THE WATER PUMP

I was overjoyed when I finally received the letter of my admission to the University of Lagos in the Big City, but I wondered how to break it to the members of my group: Alani and Tola without shattering their hearts. Already, as we were all finishing secondary school, there has been worried about all staying together and what life would be like if we all dispersed. None of us had phones like the children in the big cities do. Therefore, there was no way for us to have kept communicating except we wrote letters to each other, but even that had become so difficult.

Therefore, I held my admission letter in my hands, and I continued pondering. How would I mention it to the group? How would I say it in a way that will not break their hearts, especially Alani's? We have been friends for the longest time, and I know how much it would affect him if he discovered that I was going to leave the village. I guessed I just have to man up and tell them anyway. I told myself that and I decided to do that later that evening.

I went to the water pump as usual to get some water and when I got to the tree where we usually meet Alani and Tola were already there waiting for me. That was strange because usually, I was the most punctual of the three of us. So, when I saw both of them waiting for me, I knew something was up. When I got there and greeted them, they muttered granting greetings as though they were being forced to greet me. Surely there was something up they knew something that I didn't. Then I decided to ask my friends what was happening.

“Why are you behaving weird today?” I asked but they both stayed silent. And I wondered, “come on, what's wrong? We are friends and we shouldn't be doing this to each other.” Then Alani flared up.

“Well, maybe what you should think about is what you should not be doing to us,” Alani said.

“I don't understand what you are saying,” I replied. Alani gave Tola a knowing look and the latter shot back at me.

“No, you don't understand what we are saying indeed. Alani, please tell him we know already,” she said. Then Alani cut in.

“Adio, we already know about your admission to the university,” Alani added. I was shocked and my mouth was wide open. This was not how I planned to tell them. This was not how I wanted them to know.

“How did you find out?” I asked.

“Well, that is not yours to worry about. Maybe I found out from your younger brother. Maybe I didn't, but you don't have to worry about that,” Alani answered.

“What is really important is that you didn't even inform us you were applying to the university in the first place. Talk less of gaining admission. Did you think we could never find out?” Tola said. I didn’t know what to say.

“I am sorry. This was not how I intended everything to go,” I said with all sense of remorse.

“Oh, you are sorry? And that fixes everything? After you have tried to run away from the group. How can you be so disloyal to us when we have been together for all these years?” Alani cut in.

“I am very sorry again, this was not how I planned it to be,” I pleaded. “Tola, please. You have to understand me,” I added.

“No, I really don't understand you, Adio. This is very strange. This is not our friend that we have always known,” Tola said.

“But are you guys saying you did not apply to any university?” I asked. “Do you plan to stay in the village for the rest of your life?” I continued.

“Yes, there it is. I know you did not want to be part of us. I know you've always wanted to escape from us, that's why you are going to the big city, right?” Alani said.

“What does the big city even? Will this big city give you new friends like us?” Tola asked, and I was forced to ponder that for a moment.

"Guys, we don't have to make a mountain out of a molehill. Please try to understand where I am coming from. This was not how I intended it to be," I pleaded.

"This is how it has turned out to be. I guess we can no longer be friends. Please go your way," Alani said. He shook Tola's hand and they both left my presence while I remained by the base of the tree, wallowing in my tears at having lost my friends in this way.

CHAPTER THREE
HEARTBREAK AT THE WATER PUMP

I was worried about breaking up the group, but this was not the first and the group has had breaking up scare. Many times, we had threatened each other. We argued fiercely. But unlike the initial fight, Alani and I had, neither of us have engaged in a physical fight. Now it seems this was the worst non-physical fight we had ever gotten into because it seemed the group was broken up for good.

So imagine my surprise the following day when I went to the water pump, only to meet both of them there again. Well, apparently the group had not broken up after all. I definitely went towards them when Tola stopped me and said, "Adio, we are still angry with you from yesterday."

"Yes, we are," Alani said, corroborating her. "We are still angry with him, but we are friends. So, what do friends do? They forgive each other," he added to my surprise.

"I'm very sorry, guys," I said. "I'm really sorry and I appreciate you for forgiving me," I added?

"Now, we have to look for a way to remedy this situation. We can't let our friendship die like this, even if one of us is going to various places," said Alani.

"Yes, that is true," I said. Then I added, "Tola, what do you think?" I noticed that she was looking down at her feet, obviously shy to say something.

"I have an announcement too," Tola announced abruptly. She looked at us pleadingly with tears almost welling up from her eyes. "I am leaving for my uncle's place in one week to live with him and find work," she said.

"What is this that I am hearing?" Alani, shocked, said. "Wow, did you two plan this?" he added, facing both of us. "I know your uncle lives in Lagos, Tola, isn't that, right?" he asked.

"Yes, my uncle lives in Lagos," Tola replied.

"So you two planned this to get away from me and live happily ever after," Alani said.

"Alani, it is nothing like that," I replied, understanding how bad Alani must feel.

"If it is absolutely nothing like that, what is it like, then?" Alani said. I could feel the anger welling up in his voice. "Explain it to me," he added. "Adio, I have already known since the first day that you had your eyes on Tola. I just never knew that he could execute your plan in this treacherous manner," he said.

"Alani, please, you just have to remain calm," Tola said, placing her hands over his shoulder. "None of us planned this. These things are happening coincidentally," she added.

"And you want me to believe that?" Alani said, with the tone of his voice inching higher. "We are breaking up the group for these flimsy reasons and you want me to believe that?" he asked again.

"Alani, listen, these are not flimsy reasons. I am going to Lagos to further my education and Tola says she's leaving for Lagos to find work. These are important things. Maybe it's high time you found something to do with yourself," I cut in, having been eager to say a piece of my mind. Alani looked at me and shrugged in obvious disappointment.

"Well, it has come to this. I have now become the enemy because I am trying to save the group from ruin," Alani said. Then I realised the tone of my speech might have put him off.

"I am very sorry that is not how I meant it. That is not what I meant to say," I replied, with genuine remorse. Obviously, Alani didn't believe me.

"What did you mean to say then? I'm a useless person, right? I can't do anything for myself and I'm just going to die in the village. Isn't that what you mean?" he asked.

"No, Alani, I definitely will not disrespect my friend like that," I replied. "You are my best friend and should trust my intentions," I added

"No, I am not going to trust your intentions. You are betraying me. Why should I trust anything you say?" he asked.

"Alani, pleasc just listen to us for a moment. We can work on something else," Tola said."

"Don't worry, I am just going to die in the village," Alani said, and then he turned away.

CHAPTER FOUR
TREACHEROUS SABOTAGE

When I woke up on the day I was going to leave for Lagos, I discovered that my admission letter had been torn into shreds. I was horrified. But I know exactly who did it. I went to confront my younger brother. He was the other person apart from Alani who was angry that I was leaving the village. Although I know my younger brother's own was more of sulking, I understood that he could be unstable like that to just tear my admission letter to shreds.

"Kunle, come here. Who tore my admission letter like this?" I asked.

"I am not the one," he said, reacting even more shocked than I was. I was surprised; it was as though my brain was playing a prank on me. But if he was not going to confess to me. He was going to confess to our parents, so I went to meet them in the sitting room.

"Daddy and Mummy, Kunle tore my admission letter," I said. They both screamed "abomination!" at the same time. "It's not possible," they said.

"Ask him," I told them. But when they asked, Kunle pleadingly repeated, "I am not the one."

I got a little convinced even though, in a corner of my mind, I felt it might be his regular theatrics, but I decided to give him the benefit of the doubt. Then I realized that only one other person had access to my room. It was Alani. I ran off to his house immediately to confront him.

When I arrived at Alani's house, I met Tola and her mother there, shouting.

"Alani, come outside here. We saw you. You were the one. Come outside!" they screamed. I went to meet Tola.

"Tola, what is wrong?" I asked.

"My mother sighted Alani deflating the tire of my uncle's car who has come to pick me up to Lagos."

"What?!" I screamed. "What do you mean?"

"What about you? Tola asked. "Why are you here this early in the morning?"

"I discovered that my admission letter had been torn into shreds and I know only Alani could have done it," I answered.

"Well, you must not be serious," she said, looking even more horrified for me.

"I am very serious," I said. Then I added, "I just discovered it this morning. This boy wants to finish our lives."

We continued shouting, "Alani, come outside," but it seems the house was locked. After a few moments, his grandmother came outside to meet us and said, "why are you people disturbing me?"

“Mama, we are really sorry for disturbing you, but we have come to see your grandson,” I said. “Alani has done some terrible things and he must account for them,” I added.

“Which Alani are you talking about?” the elderly woman said.

“Mama, we are talking about your grandson here,” Tola answered.

“Alani has returned to his parents’ place early this morning. It could not have been him you saw,” the woman replied feebly. Tola fell to the ground, and I shouted, “ah! Are you serious?!”

“Yes,” the grandmother said, tired because we had been disturbing her sleep. “Yes, I am serious. Alani has returned to his parents’ house today since he has finished the secondary school education he came here for,” she answered.

“This boy has finally sabotaged us. What kind of problem is this? For God's sake!” Tola started wailing and I joined in crying. Even her mother cried with us. But the grandmother did not understand what happened. When we explained it to her, she felt very sad as well, but there was little she could do.

There was no telephone with which she could call Alani’s parents. And if she wanted to hear anything from him, she had to wait for a letter which could take weeks to arrive, even if Alani had got to his parents’ place.

A story of friendship that began at the water pump became a story of treacherous sabotage.

A LESSON IN IRONY

CHAPTER ONE

PROPHECY MADE

The bishop looked straight at his congregation, who were all silent as they awaited a powerful outburst from the pulpit. During these moments, the hall was always silent and you could even hear a pin drop if you listened carefully.
"It is time for the prophetic hour," Bishop Oyekan declared. Immediately after he uttered that, the entire hall burst into a shout. Everyone screamed for joy and was amazed at the things that were going to happen. If you had been a member of Bishop Oyekan's congregation long enough, you knew better than to joke with his prophecies. Even people who had never attended the Resurrection Church of Christ never joked whenever his prophecies went public.

When Bishop Oyekan prophesied that the former president would lose the election, many people doubted him and even left the church because they felt he was being too political. But after the prophecy got fulfilled, they all came crawling back to beg him for forgiveness.

To his members, the worst thing that could happen to you was to have Bishop Oyekan make a prophecy that was against you. Everyone knew him as 'talk and do'. And that was his nickname: Prophet Talk and Do. Even to outsiders.

Amidst the burst of noise that erupted in his congregation, Bishop Oyekan raised his right hand to signal silence. And the entire hall fell dead silent once again. Everyone waited patiently as the bishop was about to utter his prophecy. Then he started.

"I have only one word from the Lord today," Bishop Oyekan said. Everyone knew that this was to be taken seriously. During prophetic hours on Sundays like this, Bishop Oyekan would make a series of multiple prophecies on various issues. But whenever he spoke only one prophetic statement, everyone knew to take that seriously because it was definitely going to get fulfilled.

His prophecies could be compared to betting and placing a stake on certain outcomes. His prophecies were like fixed matches that you just know what was going to happen because some people higher up had already determined the outcome. That was how his members had come to depend on his prophecies. Then Bishop Oyekan continued.

"I have only one prophecy for you today and what the Lord is telling me is that there is a famous figure in this country that is going to suffer a major loss within seven days," he said. Immediately after he uttered that, there was another round of noise from the congregation.

Everyone was either shocked or amazed but there was little doubt as to who the prophecy concerned. Even outsiders knew the famous figure who had been the thorn in the flesh with Bishop Oyekan. His rift with Governor Adams, who was contesting for the position of president, was in the public gaze enough.

Governor Adams had called the bishop out a few times as one of the ministers who sell their pulpit for money. And Bishop Oyekan had retorted, saying that the governor was soon going to be destroyed. But until that moment, the bishop had never given a definitive prophecy. When Bishop Oyekan continued his speech, it turned out to be a definite reference to someone who everyone knew.

"This person I am talking about...," he said but the rowdiness of the congregation prevented him from passing the message smoothly. "Can everyone remain silent?" he asked.

Immediately, everyone was quiet again. Then he continued. "This person I am talking about is someone who has been a thorn in the flesh of the body of Christ for a long time and he is a very famous figure in this country," the bishop said. Then, it was sure that the prophecy was concerning Governor Adams.

Everywhere was noisy again until Bishop Oyekan raised his hand to signal silence before he continued. "Unless this person apologises to the body of Christ and the man of God on this mountain, then God says he shall suffer a major loss within seven days," he said.

Everyone shouted with amazement and even some were afraid for the said public figure because according to the bishop's previous prophecies, this one was likely to get fulfilled. Immediately after passing his message, Bishop Oyekan dropped the mic and went to his seat, leaving the congregation in a frenzy. They believed that it would definitely be fulfilled if Bishop Oyekan said it.

The service went on as normal without much trouble. The trouble would come later when the news would get to the TV stations. The media reported that Bishop Oyekan had prophesied that a famous figure who had been disturbing his church would suffer a major loss. It wasn't hard for anyone to draw a connection between the bishop's prophecy to his public rift with Governor Adams.

In fact, some stations reached out to Governor Adams for comments, but the latter's spokesperson said their camp did not care about what the bishop said but everything was in place to ensure the security of the governor and his family as he prepares for his presidential campaigns. He was defiant.

CHAPTER TWO
PROPHET DEFIANT

From when the prophecy was uttered on Sunday throughout the rest of the week, there were pleas from various quarters that the bishop should have mercy on Governor Adams and release him from the curse of the prophecy. Right from that Sunday evening, a group of church elders arrived at Bishop Oyekan's house to plead with him. They were led by his very assistant, Reverend Abraham.

"Please sir, we know this prophecy is referring to Governor Adams and we know that he has always been a troublemaker, but we ask you to please forgive him and release him from the curse of this prophecy. We are sure that he is going to repent and as we speak, we have sent a delegation to him as well," Reverend Abraham said, with all the elders prostrating flat on the ground in Bishop Oyekan's opulently furnished sitting room.

From the sofa upon which the bishop sat, he cleared his throat.

"My pastors and elders, please rise and sit down," he said.

"No, sir. It will be wrong for us to sit down. Please let us remain like this. We are pleading for mercy and forgiveness," Reverend Abraham said.

"I insist," Bishop Oyekan said. "I insist that you sit down because it is better that I look into the faces of all of you as I say this," he continued.

"If you insist, sir. We cannot go against your word," Reverend Abraham said. The atmosphere in the sitting room was that of complete subservience from the pastors and elders towards their bishop, Bishop Oyekan. Slowly, they all rose to their feet after the other but still refused to sit down. Bishop Oyekan motioned to them, pointing at the seats.

“Please, sit down,” Bishop Oyekan said.

“Let us stand like this, sir, please. We are not worthy to sit before your presence while we plead with you on a very important matter like this. Let us please remain standing,” Reverend Abraham said. The other pastors and elders echoed, “yes, sir. Yes, sir.”

“Well, it’s okay. If that’s what you want, that’s fine with me,” Bishop Oyekan said and they all echoed, “thank you, sir.” There was a brief silence while Bishop Oyekan looked them all in the eyes.

“Reverend Abraham. Elder Badejo,” Bishop Oyekan called and each of them replied, “sir.”

“You both have been in this church for a long time and if there’s anything you know I don’t like, it’s for people to twist my words,” Bishop Oyekan said. The pastors and elders all looked at each other, wondering what they had said wrong. But Bishop Oyekan continued. “In my prophecy, I never said it was directed towards Governor Adams or what do you call him? Did I?” he asked.

“No, sir. You did not,” the pastors and elders chorused.

“Then why have you let the media deceive you that he was the one I was talking about? I only said a major political figure will suffer loss because he has been an antagonist of this church. God did not reveal the particular person to me,” Bishop Oyekan said.

“Sir, truly, we know that you did not mention anyone’s name, but everyone knows about Governor Adams’ issues with you,” Reverend Abraham said, falling to his knees and prostrating. He only succeeded in angering his Bishop. Bishop Oyekan flared up.

“Stop it! Reverend Abraham, stop it now! Or else you will get into serious trouble!” Bishop Oyekan said. Then he continued, “I am not bothered about what anyone thinks. As a pastor, you are very close to me, and you should know better than the media that is trying to put words into my mouth. I have no business with Governor Adams and if the prophecy is about him, well, it is God that you have to ask because he’s the one who asked me to deliver the message.”

“I’m very sorry sir. We understand sir,” Reverend Abraham said.

“So if you want to plead for forgiveness and mercy on behalf of Governor Adams or anyone you think the prophecy might have been referring to, you have to direct your pleas to God, not me,” Bishop Oyekan said.

“No problem sir, we’re going to do that. Thank you, sir,” Reverend Abraham said.

“It’s okay, you can all leave my sight. I’m even feeling angry,” Bishop Oyekan said.

“We’re leaving now sir,” Reverend Abraham replied, motioning to the other pastors and elders to leave before Bishop Oyekan gets angrier.

Once they left, Bishop Oyekan’s wife, Evelyn came into the room.

"My husband, don't mind these people, they are always stressing you," she said.

"The media is just trying to twist my words. I didn't mention anyone's name. Or did I?" Bishop Oyekan said.

"No, you did not," Evelyn said. Then she continued, "but really, do you have any idea who it might have been?"

"Evelyn, you have started again, you want to behave like these people who I sent out a while ago," Bishop Oyekan said.

"No oh. I'm just asking a random question. It's okay if you don't have the answer. It doesn't really bother me, especially since you said the person is an antagonist of the church. It's only right that they are punished for their actions," she answered.

"Yes, now, you are talking," Bishop Oyekan said. "But honestly, in my mind, I feel something bad is about to befall Governor Adams. But let's see if he's going to come and beg me. He thinks that I am going to walk over to him after he embarrassed me outside," Bishop Oyekan said.

"That is beneath your status as a man of God. He's the one who has to come and beg you," his wife answered.

"Just leave him with his ignorant presidential campaign, we will see who will laugh last," Bishop Oyekan said. He and his wife let out a peal of derisive laughter.

CHAPTER THREE

PROPHECY FULFILLED?

For seven days, the pleas continued, especially in public. Many public groups came out to apologise to Bishop Oyekan for whatever Governor Adams had said to him in the past. But Bishop Oyekan was unyielding. He said his message did not refer to anybody and that if anyone knew himself to have been an antagonist of the church and was a major figure, let them apologise. But in people's minds, knowing how everyone had come to rely on Bishop Oyekan's prophecies, everyone waited eagerly until the following Sunday, when it'll be the seventh day since he issued the prophecy.

On Sunday, the church was filled to the brim. No one wanted to miss out on the action. If indeed something had happened, everyone wanted a front-row seat to know who it had happened to. The church members particularly had paid attention to the news to hear of any loss to any major figure but apparently, nothing significant happened throughout the week. News stations carried the normal campaign events and nothing seemed out of place.

However, on Sunday, when everyone had arrived at church, Bishop Oyekan was nowhere to be found. Even non-members who had come on that day to witness the spectacle of Bishop Oyekan trying to defend himself as he realises that his prophecy did not come to pass, were not granted the chance for such because he was absent. Pastors were all looking around, waiting for the service to start. After about 30 minutes of delay, a group of pastors and elders led by Reverend Abraham came up to the pulpit and they made an announcement.

"We are really sorry, Bishop Oyekan will not be with us at this moment but he is fine and okay," Reverend Abraham said. "We will carry on with the service now," he continued. Throughout the service, the programme proceeded as usual. There was singing and dancing and the scriptures were read, and prayers were offered.

Reverend Abraham preached the sermon that morning. Even news reporters who had lurked amidst the congregation were not granted the privilege of the news that they were actively hounding for. It seemed the entire nation was waiting upon the Resurrection Church of Christ to see what would happen. But at the end of the day, nothing seemed to happen. And when the service was over, which was mostly held in silence, everyone trooped out to their homes. Immediately after Reverend Abraham stepped out of the church, news reporters started asking him questions.

"Where is Bishop Oyekan? Where are his wife and his family? We didn't see them in the church today, can you explain why? Why were you the one who preached the sermon today? What do you have to say about Bishop Oyekan's prophecy? Do you still think it will be fulfilled today?" the reporters launched at him with a barrage of questions. Reverend Abraham raised his hand, motioning to them to be quiet before he spoke.

"I am not in the position to address this matter," he said. "Bishop Oyekan himself will address all of you when the time is right," he added. As he made way to push past them, the reporters continued with their questioning.

“When will the right time be? It’s been seven days since Bishop Oyekan issued the prophecy, do you think this is connected to that prophecy?” they asked.

“Please, I have told you what I know and to the best of my knowledge, Bishop Oyekan will address everyone at the right time. Please be patient and don’t stoke public tension,” Reverend Abraham cautioned.

By afternoon, all the news stations had publicised that Bishop Oyekan was nowhere to be found. Everyone started drawing analysis as to whether it was connected to the prophecy he had made. Everyone wanted the inside scoop of the story. Even church members had no idea what had happened and they kept watching their TVs to know if anything had dropped and why Bishop Oyekan did not show up in the church that day. It was very unusual of him.

Usually, whenever Bishop Oyekan did not show up in church, it was the case that he had gone to minister elsewhere. But that day, there was no news that he ministered anywhere else. Therefore, his disappearance was really strange. But everyone kept strange and knew that nothing must have happened to him. Perhaps he was having one of his personal retreats as his church members knew him to be a prayerful person.

Yet, it was confusing because his personal retreats never clashed with Sunday services. Everything was strange but everyone kept calm and continued watching.

Later in the evening, Reverend Abraham was in Bishop Oyekan’s office. Apparently, Bishop Oyekan had been holed up in his home office throughout that Sunday, not willing to come out to talk with anyone. He had occasional phone calls with his assistant, though. Then Reverend Abraham came calling.

“I am really sorry again, sir,” he said. Then he added, “do you want me to release a public statement now?” They had been discussing releasing a public statement for some time concerning the incident that occurred in the morning and Bishop Oyekan had told him to hold off. Reverend Abraham had wanted to announce it during service so that the congregation could understand. However, Bishop Oyekan claimed to not yet be in a good shape to let it be public knowledge.

“Yes, Pastor, you can give the go-ahead already. I think I’m fine if it goes public now,” Bishop Oyekan said to Reverend Abraham. However, as the latter picked up his phone, the first thing he saw was a notification from a news outlet with the headline ‘Bishop Oyekan LOSES HIS SON’.

“What!?” Reverend Abraham screamed. “How did the news get out already?!” Bishop Oyekan was also too shocked to say anything. The news was out already.

“You mean someone betrayed me?” Bishop Oyekan screamed, banging the table. Reverend Abraham nodded fearfully and continued to read the news.

“Bishop Oyekan loses his son after prophesying a major loss on an unnamed popular political figure.”

A TALE OF FAILURE

CHAPTER ONE

SPEAK OF THE DEVIL

As the phone rang, Emmanuel angrily picked it up, muttering, “oh God” in anger that someone interrupted his video game. But when he checked the phone, he noticed that the caller was his best friend, Johnson. He was relieved a bit and then said “Hello Johnson, what's up now?”

“I'm good man, How are you doing?” Johnson asked.

“I'm alright,” Emmanuel replied. “I'm just playing a video game here,” he added.

“You and this your video games, eh,” Johnson teased. “Anyway, I just wanted to let you know that the UTME results are out,” he added.

“Ah, so quickly?” Emmanuel exclaimed. He didn’t expect that the results would be out so soon.

“Yes, how long did you think it was going to take? It was a computer-based test. So, they marked it very quickly,” Johnson answered.

“I don't think I am prepared to check my result though. To be honest with you, I'm not so sure of how I'm going to perform,” Emmanuel replied.

"Don’t worry, it's going to be fine,” Johnson encouraged him.

“Have you checked your own?” Emmanuel asked.

“Yes, I have. I had 257,” Johnson answered, and Emmanuel could notice the ecstasy in his voice.

“Wow, that's very good. I'm really happy for you,” Emmanuel said.

“I am just happy because my father promised me a bicycle if I score more than 250. So, I'm going to meet
him now to ask for my prize," Johnson said.

“Ah, I can't wait to see you in your new bicycle,” replied Emmanuel. “Congratulations bro,” he added.

“Well you two, go check yours, please. It should already be out,” Johnson said

“How can I check it? I don't know the way to check it,” Emmanuel answered.

“Just text JAMB RESULT to 2225566 with the phone number you used to register for your JAMB exam and it's going to bring out your results,” said Johnson.

“So quickly?” Emanuel asked.

“Yes,” Johnson replied. “What do you even know, you this boy? You are just asking questions as if we did not do the exams together,” Johnson replied.

"No vex, this video game is on my mind,” Emmanuel said.

"Don’t worry, you can go back to your video game but quickly check. Check it now," Johnson said.

"No wahala, I will check it now," Emmanuel answered. Then he cut the call. Once he dropped the call, Emmanuel could not get back to his video game as his heart started pounding. He didn't expect to have performed well in his exams and the palpitations in his heart arose because he did not know what his fate was going to be. So, for the next couple of minutes, he continued contemplating whether to check the results then or later. Then he muttered to himself, "I hope my dad has not found out yet, because he's going to make me check it almost immediately." Just as he said that his father called from the sitting room.

"Emmanuel!" he shouted.

Emmanuel muttered "speak of the devil" and banged his palm on his forehead, saying "I knew it. That man already knows, as if he's a wizard or something." So, at first, he didn't answer.

"Emmanuel. Are you in there?" His father called out again.

Emmanuel knew he had not much time to fake not having heard the person calling him, so he screamed back, "I am. Yes, I am coming, dad." Slowly and in trepidation. He walked towards his sitting room where his father was seated watching cable news.

CHAPTER TWO

CHOKED UP

"Emmanuel, I am just seeing from the news now that JAMB has released its results," his father said. As Emmanuel was not ready to check anything yet, he faked ignorance.
"Oh, dad, is that so?" He asked.
"Yes, it is true. The newscaster just reported it now. Why don't you check your own right away?" His father said.
"I am not sure if they are released. I have not heard the news from any of my friends if they have checked theirs," Emmanuel answered, doing all he could to avoid checking his results before his father.

"Don't worry, you check yours first and let's at least confirm if the news is true. Type the code that is on the TV to your phone so that it can display your results," his father answered.

"Okay, dad," Emmanuel replied. Then he sat down, far away from his father, so if his results turned out so badly, he would not be close enough for his father to hit him. Slowly he typed the code numbers one after the other and sent them to the JAMB USSD code.

"Have you checked it?" his father asked with Emmanuel peering at his phone intently. He was suspicious that his son wasn't going to telling the truth.

"No, I have not gotten a response yet," Emmanuel said. Indeed, he had not gotten a response, but the tension in his voice made it seem like he was lying.

"Emmanuel, are you lying to me?" His father asked.

"No, dad. I am not lying to you. Why would I lie to you?" Emmanuel replied. No one said anything for a moment, but his father continued looking at him with suspicion. After a few minutes, his father was fed up with the tension.

"Emmanuel, bring me your phone," he said, stretching out his palm to collect the phone from his son and Emmanuel handed over the phone immediately. He watched as his father entered the code by himself and sent it out to the JAMB centre. Then he waited and there were still no results.

"Emmanuel, I have not gotten any response from this service yet," he said.

"Well, I told you it's not yet out, the newscaster is just reporting their own," Emmanuel answered, relieved that he had successfully postponed the evil day.

"Okay, no problem," Emmanuel's father replied, handing over the phone to his son. "But let me just warn you. If you should fail that exam, that would be the end of your journey in life because I know that you never prepared well for the exam in the first place, so I'm not expecting the best results from you," His father added. Emmanuel bowed his head, having expected this coding

'At least this man would have kept this scolding until he had seen the results," Emmanuel thought.

"You know, I have always told you I can't take anything from any of my children. But not poor academic performance, but that is exactly what you have only shown. Your academic results have always been poor. If you fail this JAMB exam, there is no future for you, just know that you are going to be on the streets, doing nonsense up and down. Whenever we tell you to read your books, you never read your books. You never study. You are always playing video games," his father continued schooling. "Once you get the results, you must make sure you tell me, is that okay?" he asked.

"No problem, dad, I will do so," Emmanuel said. Just as he stood up to go to his room, his mother emerged from the kitchen where she had been cooking.

"Has Emmanuel checked his results yet? I heard you talking about it," She asked her husband.

"JAMB said the results are out as I saw in the news now, but I just tried to check Emmanuel's without response yet. Let's wait for a few days," he replied. Then Emmanuel's mother turned towards the boy. "No problem, I guess we can wait for a few days but Emmanuel, I am not expecting the best from you at all because you did not prepare well for that exam. But let's see. If you fail that exam, just know that no school for you again, so you better go to your room now and start praying that you come out with an excellent result," she added.

Emmanuel hung his head in shame again. Every day, he has always endured snide remarks about his performance in school, and his struggles with grades. He knew it wasn't going to end soon, but he expected his parents to be more supportive, especially since they had not even seen the results yet. They didn't know how bad it is yet if it was.

"No problem," Emmanuel man said. Then he went to his room.

CHAPTER THREE

ANXIETY

For the rest of the day, Emmanuel was filled with anxiety over the results of his exam. He kept checking at various times during the day because he could not take his mind off it. He could not even focus his attention on the video game he loves so much.

The following day, immediately Emmanuel woke up, the first thing he did was check his result. At the time he opened his phone to check, he was half awake. But when the notification came in that he scored 132 in JAMB, he jolted fully awake immediately, shocked at what he was saying, and he peered at it intensely again. Right away, a call came in that made him shriek wildly. It was his friend Johnson.

“Hey, Emmanuel, what's up?” Johnson said.

"Oh, Johnson, it's you. I’m okay,” Emmanuel answered, still trying to struggle from sleep with his croaky voice.

“Emmanuel, how far? You didn't get back to me yesterday. Did you later check your results?” Johnson said. Not knowing what to reply to his friend, Emmanuel kept quiet. Johnson thought it was the network that was misbehaving.

“Emmanuel are you there?” he repeated.

“Yes, Johnson I checked actually and well, I don't know how to put this, but I failed. I had 132,” Emmanuel answered. Johnson went silent for a moment at the mention of Emmanuel’s score.

“Emmanuel, are you there with me?” Johnson asked

“Yes, I am. I'm with you, Johnson,” Emmanuel said.

“Don't worry, it's going to be fine. Okay? Do you hear me? it's going to be fine,” Johnson replied.

“Well, I don't think it's going to be fine. My parents have been threatening me since yesterday over my results, so I don't think your motivational speeches are going to work for me,” Emmanuel said.

"Well, I wasn't trying to motivate you, but at least just keep up hope,” Johnson said. “Do you understand?” he added. “I'll call you later in the day. I need to get out now.”

"Oh, no problem. I appreciate your support. I will figure out a way to tell my parents,” Emmanuel answered.

Throughout the day, Emmanuel Immanuel stayed locked up in his room, not even coming out during the family devotion when everyone gathered to pray. After the devotion, Emmanuel’s father turned to him and said, “Emmanuel, have you tried checking the result against his yesterday?

“Yes, I have, dad,” he answered.

"And what is it that he is that you scored, you dullard?” his father asked.

"Dad, I have not seen my results yet. I don't know. I think there might be a problem somewhere,” Emmanuel said.

“Emmanuel, with the way this is going, I hope you didn't cheat in that exam and they caught you,” his father asked. Emmanuel was shocked.

“How come? No, dad,” he said, looking around with confusion. Then his mother decided to chip in.

“Yes, that’s true. I hear that they do withdraw the result of students that have been found to cheat. And I'm not putting that past you, Emmanuel. You have always been wayward like that,” his mother said.

CHAPTER FOUR

THE FAILURE

"No, mum. No, dad. That's not possible. I could never cheat on my exams," Emmanuel answered. His parents looked at him with confusion, then his father decided to break the silence.

"I don't even care about that. Whatever you do with your life is none of my business. I have tried my best over you already, so if it is the case that you cheated and you were caught, it is your life to live. What is my business?" his father said.

"No, dad. I didn't cheat. I don't know. Not everyone among my classmates has even seen their results yet," Emmanuel answered.

"No problem," his mother said. Then she added, "but what about those who have seen it? What did your friend Johnson score?"

Emmanuel was mute for a moment until his father tapped him and said, "Emmanuel, don't hear what your mother is asking you? Who did your friend score?"

"Two fifty-seven," Emmanuel said.

"That's a wonderful result," his mother answered. "I know that boy's parents will be so proud of him, but you, I can't say as much. That boy has always performed excellently well and he reads his books too, unlike you," his mother added. As he had always done, whenever his parents were scolding him, Emanuel hung his head in shame until he decided to speak out.

"But dad and mum, you have not even seen my results yet and they are making such conclusions. At least let me see it first. What if I pass?" Emmanuel said. His father laughed and his mother joined in the laughter too.

"Emmanuel, you pass? When have you ever passed an exam? You are such a lazy dullard, so please don't disturb me with that. I have simply told you what I'm going to do. If you fail that exam. I'm going to take you somewhere to learn mechanic or something because school is not for you. That is what you have been telling me," his father said.

To that, Emmanuel had no response but to keep silent and watch as his parents made jest of him as though they weren't his parents. As though they were outsiders. He felt his heart being pulled apart to hear his parents' making remarks about him in such a vile way. All his life he had never felt like he had the support of his parents due to his struggles in school. Of course, they were proud of his other siblings.

Esther was a highflier in her class and even though she was his youngest sister, his parents always used her as a point of comparison to him. “Why can't you be like Esther?” They would always say.

On the older side, his brother, Daniel was the best student in his secondary school and his results from university showed that he was in first-class. His parents would often tell him whenever they called Daniel in school.

“Daniel, speak with your brother. He should be more like you. Emmanuel doesn't read. Emmanuel doesn't study.” And then Emanuel will protest, “dad, I try, I try to read.”

But his parents continued to react toward him with hate, often retorting with “Emmanuel, you don’t try. You should read better. You should study better,”

But Emmanuel would often protest with his struggles. How he struggles to make out words. How he struggles to learn and how he struggles to understand what other people are saying. Because of his learning difficulties, Emmanuel has turned to video games, which are his refuge. He knows he doesn't have to take an exam for a video game. He just must beat his opponents in the matches.

But even that, his parents would never let him be. They could never understand why they had a son who was so anti-school and who never wanted to study anything. Maybe they will later.

Or maybe it was too late, but at least the least they could do was to show him, Emmanuel, some love which he was so clearly lacking in his life.

Throughout the day, his parents continued to make snide remarks at Emmanuel. When it was night, his mother lovingly called him and said "Emmanuel, my son. Your dinner is ready." But when Emmanuel came out and started eating, the same mother was the one to say "why do you eat so much? If you loved your books the same way you love eating, wouldn't you be much better than this?" At that point, the food turned sour in Emmanuel's mouth and when he could no longer continue, his father said, "so you can soberly reflect on your foot eating habits, but you can't find a place to reflect on your school performances? Just let your JAMB results come out first and you will see what happens then.

EPILOGUE

The following day, Emmanuel was found lifeless in his room, having hung himself.

ABOUT THE AUTHOR

Abiodun Felix Taiwo is an illustrious entrepreneur. He bagged his OND and HND degree in Statistics from The Polytechnic Ibadan. He later b a g g e d a n o t h e r d e g r e e i n Computer science from Achievers University in Owo, Ondo State. He went ahead to study at Leeds Becket University, United Kingdom, where he bagged a degree in Entrepreneurship and Business Development, because of his passion for improvement and international experience.

He is a co-founder of Desam Oil and Gas Ltd. with his wife for a decade in Lagos, Nigeria. Abiodun is a co-founder of STONE Foundation, registered in Nigeria, a charity organization which is helping the ORPHANS (It's aimed at helping the children of the Nigerian Army personnel who lost their breadwinners in North-Eastern part of Nigeria, where Boko-Haram is ravaging war against western education). He is also a loving and caring father with great passion for children and he is a strong believer of Christ

www.ingramcontent.com/pod-product-compliance
Lightning Source LLC
LaVergne TN
LVHW050348160826
845677LV00014B/3864

9798846890350